AMY TAN

The Chinese Siamese Cat

illustrated by GRETCHEN SCHIELDS

MACMILLAN PUBLISHING COMPANY   NEW YORK
Maxwell Macmillan Canada   Toronto
Maxwell Macmillan International   New York   Oxford   Singapore   Sydney

For Sagwa and Sluggo

Text copyright © 1994 by Amy Tan. Illustrations copyright © 1994 by Gretchen Schields.
All rights reserved. No part of this book may be reproduced or transmitted in any form or by any means, electronic
or mechanical, including photocopying, recording, or by any information storage and retrieval system, without
permission in writing from the Publisher. Macmillan Publishing Company is part of the Maxwell Communication
Group of Companies. Macmillan Publishing Company, 866 Third Avenue, New York, NY 10022. Maxwell
Macmillan Canada, Inc., 1200 Eglinton Avenue East, Suite 200, Don Mills, Ontario M3C 3N1. First edition.
Printed in Hong Kong.
10   9   8   7   6   5   4   3   2   1

Library of Congress Catalog Card Number: 93-24008
ISBN 0-02-788835-5

When her five kittens were eight weeks old and ready for new homes, Ming Miao called her brood together one last time.

"Before you go out into the world," she said, "you must know the true story of your ancestors."

Four pairs of light brown kitten ears twitched and pointed toward their mother, eager to listen. But a fifth pair of ears was turned toward a lizard that was scampering under a nearby rock.

"The truth is," Ming Miao began, "you are not Siamese cats but Chinese cats. As a matter of fact, one of our family's ancestors from a thousand cat lives ago was the famous feline Sagwa of China. She's the reason your faces, ears, paws, and tails will turn darker and darker. She's the reason I taught you to say politely in Chinese *miao-miao-miao* instead of *mee-yow-OW*, the cranky way Siamese cats do when they cry for their food."

Four kittens licked themselves proudly. But one kitten—guess which one—was now busy swatting under a muddy rock with her light brown paw, searching for the lizard. And so she was not really paying attention as Ming Miao told her kittens the story of their great ancestor, Sagwa of China. . . .

Sagwa was one of three pearl white kittens born to Mama Miao and Baba Miao, two fine cats who lived in a place everyone called the House of the Foolish Magistrate. The Foolish Magistrate was in charge of issuing rules and proclamations for the people and animals of his province.

If he had been a wise magistrate, he would have thought up rules to make others happy and healthy. A wise magistrate would have ordered people to care for cats who were sick or without homes. A *very* wise magistrate would have proclaimed that all cats should eat catfish every day.

But he was not wise. He made up rules that helped only himself. Because he wanted to command respect, he ordered people and animals to bow down to him. Because he was afraid people laughed at him behind his back, he made up a rule that people could no longer laugh. Because he wanted more money, he charged people fines for breaking his rules.

And since the Magistrate had made so many rules, people had to pay him many fines. Which is why he had a lot of money. Which is why his house grew to have many lavish rooms and courtyards. Which is why there were many places that little kittens could explore and where they could get themselves into many kinds of trouble.

The kittens were as round and fat as melons. In fact, they were named Dongwa, which means "winter melon," Sheegwa, which means "watermelon," and Sagwa, which means "melon head."

Actually, "melon head" was another way of saying "silly," which is what Sagwa was known to be. She scampered into vases and knocked them down. She clawed her way up banners and pulled them down.

She walked on the rims of giant fishbowls, and she was the one who fell down—*pwah!*—right into the water.

In other words, Sagwa was the kind of cat who always found her way into trouble—not on purpose, of course.

Other than that, she was just like all the cats in the Miao family.

The cats were born with creamy white fur all over, the same color as fine scroll paper. Over the years, however, the tails of Mama Miao and Baba Miao had turned the color of lampblack ink. That was because of the hard work that the Foolish Magistrate had them do.

You see, he had discovered that the pointy-tipped tails of cats made very fine writing brushes. That's what the Magistrate used for writing his silly rules: the tails of Mama Miao and Baba Miao. He dipped them into a pot of lampblack Chinese ink, the kind of ink that doesn't wash off.

Mama Miao and Baba Miao were very smart—as are all the cats in our family—and soon they did not need the Magistrate to guide their tails. They knew how to write the words all by themselves. Of course, the Magistrate still told them what they should write: No dancing! No playing! No celebrating!

One day, the Foolish Magistrate called Mama Miao and Baba Miao to his study as usual. It was a large, cold room filled with bookshelves, poem paintings, and carved window screens painted red and gold. There, the Magistrate sat in his big dragon chair, already tapping his fingers impatiently as the two cats arrived to do his dirty work.

Now, if you're thinking there were only two cats in the room, think again. High up on a shelf was the kitten Sagwa, who thought a dark spot between dusty books was the perfect place for a catnap.

But when Sagwa heard the Magistrate shouting for her parents, she woke up—in time to watch and hear everything from her secret perch.

First, Mama Miao and Baba Miao had to jump onto the Magistrate's desk. From a cubbyhole,

Baba Miao pulled out a roll of paper tied up with a purple silk ribbon. Mama Miao pulled on the ribbon with her teeth to untie it, then sat on one end of the paper to hold it still while Baba Miao rolled the paper out with his paws. He had to be very careful not to rip the scroll with his sharp claws.

Now the Magistrate was ready to begin. "Today's new rule!" he shouted. And Baba Miao had to quickly dip his tail into the ink pot and poise himself, ready to write down the dreaded words.

"From now on," cried the Magistrate, "people must *not* sing until the sun goes down!" You see, the Magistrate believed that if people sang while they worked, they enjoyed their work. And if they enjoyed their work, well, of course, they must not be working hard enough.

"And now," he continued, "here are the names of those who broke the rule today!" And it was Mama Miao's turn to write down the names of those poor people who didn't yet know there was a rule against singing.

The Magistrate examined the cats' work, grunted his approval, then left the scroll on the table to dry. When he was gone, Mama Miao's whiskers twitched with fury.

"This rule is the worst," she hissed to Baba Miao. "Look, he's even fined the cook, just because she sang while feeding us tasty scraps for our breakfast. It's not fair."

"Yes, many things in life are not fair," said Baba Miao. "But we're only cats. We're helpless. We have no power to change the world."

And then the kitten Sagwa watched her parents walk out of the room, swishing their tails back and forth with unhappiness.

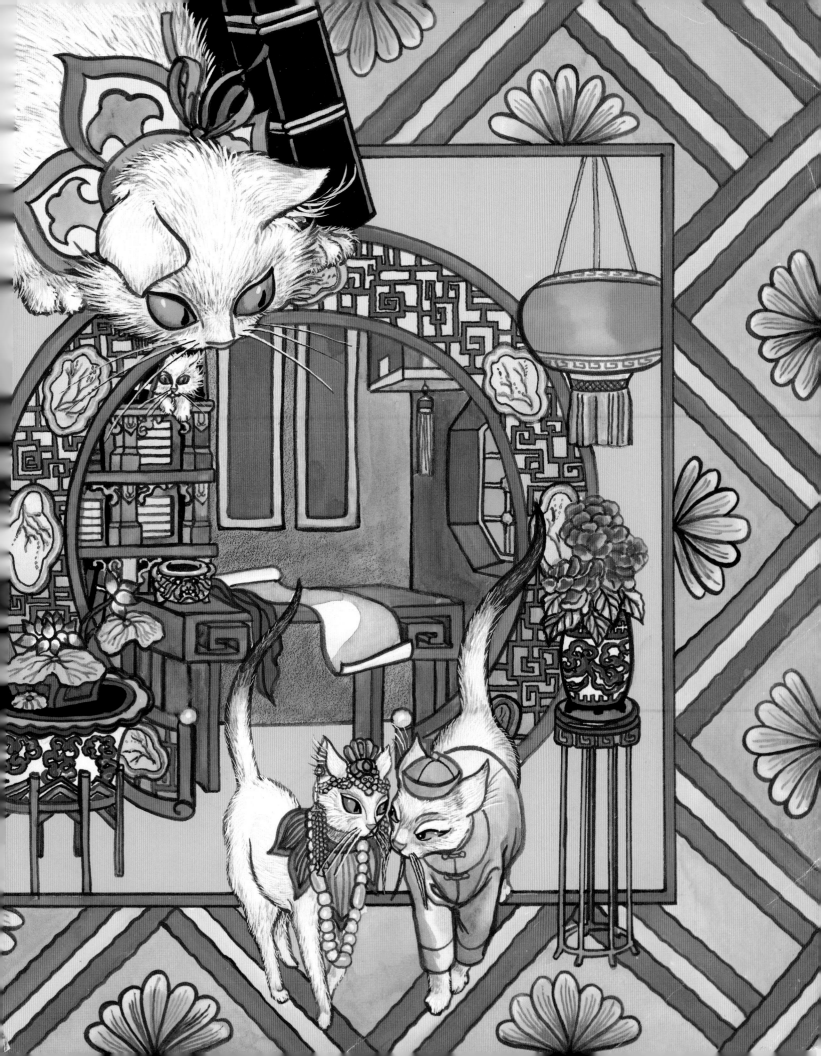

She wanted to jump down and follow them. She wanted to cry out to them, "We're not helpless. We can change the world." But then she saw how high up she was, how helpless she was herself. Far down below was the Magistrate's desk, with the Scroll of Rules lying next to the ink pot.

Finally she realized: Leap she must. There was no other choice.

Guess where she landed.

Pwah!

That's right—in the ink pot. Chinese ink flew all over her face and ears,
coating them brown-black. For a moment, she could not see, and
in her haste, she wiped her nose against
the piece of paper below her paws.
Guess what that piece of paper was.
Oh yes, the Scroll of Rules.

At first, Sagwa was quite afraid because of the mess she had made. Then she saw exactly what she had done. Her nose had accidentally blotted out the word *not*. So where the rule had once said:

"People must *not* sing until the sun goes down," now it said:

"People must sing until the sun goes down."

They *must* sing—what a delightful rule! Sagwa purred just to think of it: thousands of people singing, all that happy music.

And then Sagwa had another thought. She dipped her tail into the ink pot and sat down at the end of the sentence, making a big, fat exclamation point! Now they must really sing—loud, happy songs!

Soon enough, she saw what else she should do. She dipped all four paws into the ink pot, then danced over the names of people who were supposed to be fined for breaking the no-singing rule. She danced and danced, turning all the names into black spots that looked like happy musical notes.

Satisfied with her secret work, Sagwa jumped off the desk. She was heading out to the courtyard to lie in the rays of the morning sun when suddenly she looked to the side and saw a scary sight. It was a strange kitten. Its face and ears were black, as were its paws and tail.

Sagwa bent her ears back and hissed—and the strange kitten did the same thing at the same time. Puzzled, she sat up and cocked her head. The strange kitten did the same thing. She reached over to bat the kitten in a friendly way—and that's when Sagwa discovered she was looking at herself in a mirror.

Now she was scared for another reason. If the Magistrate saw her covered with ink, he would know what she had done. He would have her mother and father hung up by their tails for raising such a naughty kitten. He would kick the kittens out of the house. She'd heard terrible stories of homeless kittens who had to chase flies for their supper. Her whole family would suffer. And she was to blame.

Sagwa began to shiver with fright and shame. She hid behind the leg of the Magistrate's dragon chair to await her family's doom. We will be thrown to the dogs, she miaoed to herself.

Suddenly, she heard a loud knock at the door. The Official Reader of Rules had arrived. It was his job to take the scroll, read it aloud at the noon hour for all to hear, then post the new rule in the middle of the town square.

"You're two minutes late," said the Magistrate. And because he was busy eating a bowl of noodles, he told the Reader of Rules to go into the study and fetch the scroll himself.

Sagwa watched the Reader of Rules walk up to the desk. She saw his eyebrows draw together in a frown as he read the scroll. He then rolled up the scroll and marched quickly out of the room.

Of course, Sagwa
didn't know that the Reader of Rules
hated his job. He hated reading rules that made
everyone hate him as much as they hated the Magistrate.
And so when the Reader of Rules saw the new rule about
singing, he was puzzled at first, then overjoyed. On his way to the
town square, he began to sing, just as the scroll

instructed him. And when
he reached the town square at noon, he was still
singing. He sang out the new rule. From the
crowd came a great roar of disbelief.

"It's true," sang the Reader of Rules. "See
right here. We must sing until the sun goes
down."

People pressed forward to read the
scroll—once, twice, thrice. It
must be true. And then they,
too, began to sing. Songs from
their childhood. Songs about
a good harvest. Songs of
undying friendship. Songs
of love.

They took to the streets with dogs barking and donkeys braying. They ran all the way to the Magistrate's house, singing at the top of their lungs.

"What's this?" cried the Magistrate. He looked up from his bowl of noodles. He could hear the people singing, softly at first from a distance, then louder and louder as the crowd drew near.

The Magistrate ran through the courtyard, shouting, "How dare they disobey my rule!" Hearing this, Sagwa curled herself into a small, miserable ball.

Soon enough, the Magistrate was standing at his front gate, counting the number of people he would have to fine for singing: "One thousand thirty-two, one thousand thirty-three…"

He stopped when he saw the Reader of Rules in the crowd. He beckoned him over.

"Why are all these people singing?" asked the Magistrate. "Didn't you show them my new rule?"

"But this is your rule," sang back the Reader of Rules.

"*My* rule?" said the Magistrate. "Let me see."

The Reader of Rules ran back to the town square to fetch the Scroll of Rules. And when he brought it back, the Magistrate saw the lampblack ink spots and noticed how they looked just like little cat paws.

He was trying to decide how he should punish the cats, but he could not hear himself think. Those awful, happy songs the people were singing!

And then—wonder of wonders—he heard the words to the songs. They were songs in praise of him! Songs that thanked him for thinking of them. What a strange feeling he had. In all his many years as a Magistrate, he had never heard a kind word said about him, let alone songs honoring him for being kind.

Before he could stop himself, his eyes grew wet. And because he had not cried in many, many years, his heart had become thirsty and cold. How wonderful to finally fill it with warm tears of joy.

Just as the Magistrate had ordered, the singing did not stop until the sun went down. When the people finally left, the Magistrate walked back into his house, taking with him his Scroll of Rules. He went into his study and sat in his dragon chair, underneath which a little cat was still hiding.

Of course, Sagwa had not seen what had happened outside the front gate. So she was still shivering with fright. Which is why she sneezed—*chh! chh! chh!*

"Who's this?" said the Magistrate. He looked under the dragon chair and drew out the scared kitten. He immediately saw the dark spots on Sagwa's fur. He held the sad little kitten close to his face.

"So you're the one who changed my rule," he said.

And poor Sagwa squeaked, "*Miao,*" for like all cats, she didn't know how to lie. She hoped the Magistrate would punish only her, and not her mother and father. But the next thing she heard was the Magistrate calling: "Mama Miao! Baba Miao! Come here quickly!"

When they ran into the room, the Magistrate held the curled kitten high up in the air, then pointed to the Scroll of Rules. "Look what your kitten has done," he said. And Mama Miao and Baba Miao jumped onto the desk to see. Their ears flattened back in fear, and they hung their heads.

"Because of what Sagwa has done," continued the Magistrate, "I want you to write three new Scrolls of Rules."

Mama Miao and Baba Miao dipped their tails into the ink pot, ready to do their duty.

"For the first new rule," began the Magistrate, "I take back all the old rules. The people may now laugh and joke and dance and whistle from morning to night, from night to morning, whenever they desire."

Mama Miao chirped with surprise as Baba Miao wrote this down.

"As to the second new rule," said the Magistrate, "from now on, my house shall be open to all stray cats. And all cats shall eat catfish, as much as they wish."

Baba Miao purred as Mama Miao quickly wrote down this wise new rule.

"As to the third new rule," said the Magistrate, "from now on, all Chinese cats shall have dark faces, ears, paws, and tails—in honor of the greatest of felines, Sagwa of China."

"*Miao-miao-miao*," cried Sagwa, for she couldn't believe her ink-dark ears. And in her joy, she tumbled out of the Magistrate's arms and landed— well, guess where.

Right in the pot of Chinese ink…

"That's the story of our ancestors," said Ming Miao to her kittens. "If you have kittens someday, you must tell them the story of the Miao family. You must always remember—"

And then she stopped, for there was still one kitten who wasn't listening. So Ming Miao went over and grabbed the kitten's tail with her teeth and dragged her away from the muddy rock. And when the wayward kitten faced her brothers and sisters, they could all see that her face and ears and paws were brown-black with mud.

"You must always remember," Ming Miao continued, pointing her paw at the naughty kitten. "This is why we look like Siamese cats but are really Chinese cats. For better or worse, we can't help sticking our noses into trouble. Just like this kitten. Just like our ancestor,   Sagwa of China."